Jan Richardson

1997

# TAG-ALONG TIMOTHY

# TOURS ALASKA

By

## Jean Richardson

**Illustrated by Jo Ann Edington**

EAKIN PRESS ★ Austin, Texas

*With special thanks to my mother,*
*Mary Carey, and my aunt, Lela Lloyd,*
*. . . they led the way;*
*and to my daughter Linda,*
*Timothy's "real" mother.*

FIRST EDITION

Copyright © 1989
By Jean Richardson

Published in the United States of America
By Eakin Press, P.O. Box 23069, Austin, Texas 78735

ISBN 0-89015-706-5

**Library of Congress Cataloging-in-Publication Data**

Richardson, Jean.
    Tag-along Timothy tours Alaska / by Jean Richardson : illustrated by Jo
Ann Edington.
        p.        cm.
    Summary: The adventures of Tag-Along Timothy, a rabbit who loves to
travel, as he takes a trip from his home in Texas to far-off Alaska.
    ISBN 0-89015-706-5 : $10.95
    [1. Rabbits — Fiction.  2. Voyages and travel — Fiction.  3. Alaska-Fic-
tion.]    I. Edington, Jo Ann, ill.    II. Title.
PZ7.R39485Tag      1989
[E]--dc19                                                                88-36418
                                                                              CIP
                                                                              AC

# ABOUT THE AUTHOR

A native Texan, Jean Richardson holds a B.S. degree in elementary education from The University of Texas at Austin. Since graduation she has taught school in seven states, and is currently employed by the Spring Branch (Houston, Texas) School District. She is the mother of three children and is active in several community organizations. Jean has traveled to Alaska many times to visit her mother, a prolific Alaskan author. Combining her interests of travel and photography, she has taken hundreds of snapshots of Alaskan scenery, some of which were used to illustrate this book. She and her husband Frank have lived in Houston for the past twenty years.

# ABOUT THE ARTIST

Jo Ann Edington is a self-taught artist who is originally from Pennsylvania. She moved to Houston in 1976 and worked in the oil industry for ten years as a graphic artist and geophysical technician. She has been involved in many projects including pencil and oil portraits, personalized greeting cards, wall murals, sculpting, and floral arrangements. Jo Ann is married and is the mother of one daughter. She is involved in her local church, along with her work as a free-lance artist.

# TAG-ALONG TIMOTHY TOURS ALASKA

Tag-Along Timothy was hopping along a Texas trail looking for something good to eat. He had already hopped past the valley, where he usually ate clover with his five brothers and sisters. Today he was in the mood for something different. He didn't want to stop until he found it. He was tired of just tagging along with everyone else.

He was so hungry that he was about to
give up and gnaw the bark on the nearest tree.
Then he saw something interesting. A truck
had stopped on the side of the road just below
the bank where he was feeding. In the back he
could see crates, boxes, and bags full of carrots,
lettuce, cabbage, turnips, and beets. These were
all things that rabbits love to eat. He gave a
giant hop and landed right between a crate of
lettuce and a big bag of radishes.

He began to nibble, trying to taste just
about everything. What a wonderful meal!
Suddenly, the truck lurched and began to move
down the road. Timothy didn't even care. He
was having such a good time.

Timothy liked riding and nibbling. He watched all sorts of interesting things go whizzing past his crate.

He sniffed smells he had never smelled before. Some were not so good.

Soon he was passing beautiful hills of flowers. Timothy loved flowers. He wanted to stop, but the truck never even slowed down.

Timothy thought about his brothers and sisters at home. They were probably wondering why he wasn't tagging along as usual. He must

try to remember every sight and sound and smell. Wouldn't they be surprised to hear all about his incredible adventure? They would probably never tease him or call him "Tag-Along" again.

Finally, the truck stopped and two men
began unloading the crates. Timothy hid in a
crate of carrots and continued to nibble. He
chewed very quietly. The men didn't even
notice him when they carried his crate onto a
big airplane. Timothy was so full by then that
he just patted his happy little tummy and
curled into a ball. Soon he fell asleep.

Timothy slept and slept.

When he woke up, everything looked different. Should he go home now? NO! He was having too much fun. He ducked his fuzzy ears under the carrots. He closed his eyes tightly, so no one could see him. He felt the crate being lifted up and carried away.

BAM! BAM! BAM! Timothy was startled by a terrible racket. He peeped out through a crack in the crate and looked all around. He was in a big, white room with a long table. Some men dressed in white were washing the vegetables and chopping them up with shiny, long knives. This was no place for a bunny!

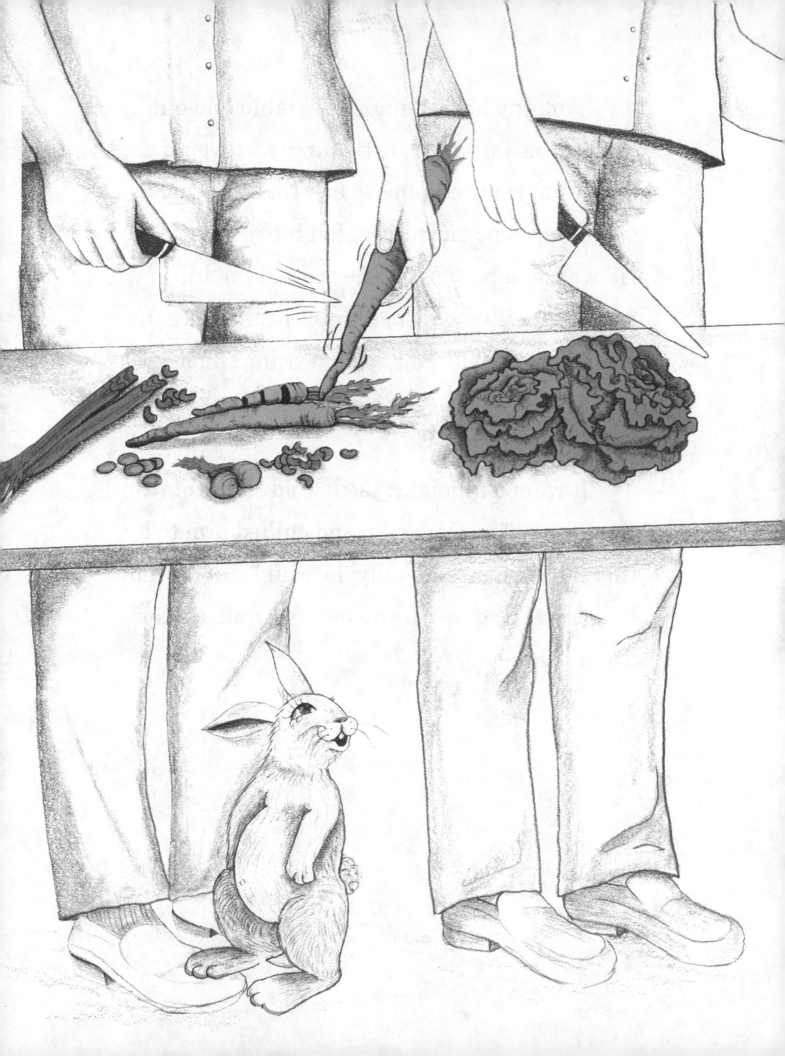

Timothy hopped under the table and out the door as fast as his little furry feet would take him. He was going so fast that he tripped over a big rope and almost fell into deep water. He was on a boat! When he spotted the hills getting smaller and smaller in the distance, he realized what big trouble he was in. Timothy crept under the edge of a big, green tarp and began to cry.

It rained all night. Little cold rivers of rain ran under Timothy's tarp and chilled him to his tiny bunny bones. Finally, he could stand it no longer. He had to venture out and find a drier place to hide.

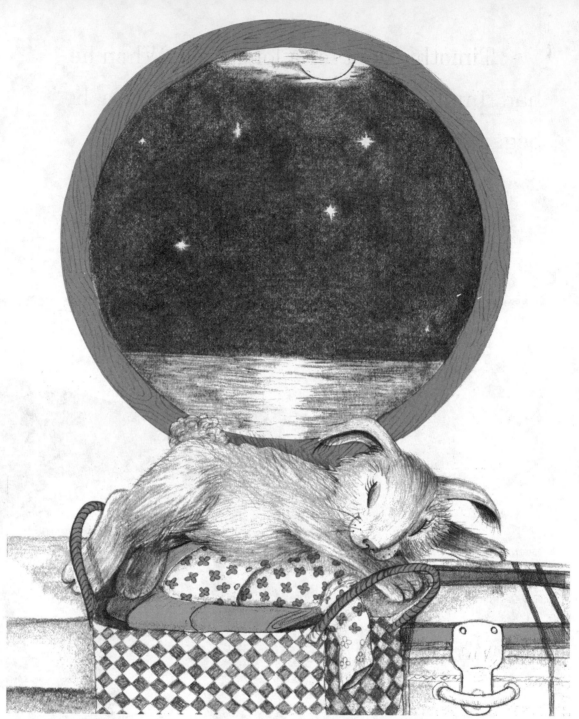

He went down some halls and through some doors. Then he found the perfect spot. It was warm and dark.

No one would ever find him here. He carefully cleaned all the rain from his fur, gave a tiny sigh of relief, and settled down for a nice nap.

Timothy slept for a long time. When he had finally rested from his terrible scare, he began to explore.

A nice little white-haired lady was sharing his stateroom. Timothy didn't mind because she was very quiet. Her straw bag full of sweaters was where he liked to sleep. She spent most of every day on the deck, looking at the scenery.

That gave Timothy lots of free time.
During the day he could see all sorts of
incredible sights out the funny round window.

Timothy liked the gentle rocking of the boat. When he got hungry, he would sneak back to the kitchen and nibble on scraps. Just as he was really beginning to enjoy sailing, the boat came to a stop. The big engines were quiet.

# Anchorage Welcomes You

Timothy barely had time to hop into his hiding place before he was lifted up and whisked away.

He wondered where he was going now. How he wished he could read the signs.

Tag-Along Timothy thought he should go home now. But before he could hop out, his bag was carried onto a tour bus.

The lady took Timothy's bag all the way to the back of the bus. She dropped Timothy on top of some other luggage. Then she went to sit near the front. Poor Timothy was bruised and shaken. He could hardly get his breath. He was

afraid someone might come and sit on him! But luckily for Timothy, everyone wanted to sit near the front so they could hear the tour guide. Timothy was all alone on the back seat.

It took Timothy a long time to get up enough courage to stick his head out and look around again. He finally decided it was safe to take one quick peek. Through the big back window he could see the city they were leaving. Up ahead he could see only trees and mountains. It did not look like Texas to him.

Timothy curled down between the boxes and suitcases and tried not to be afraid. He could smell the gasoline fumes from the engine and hear the tour guide talking. But mostly he could hear his hungry tummy telling him it was time to eat. At long last the bus stopped and all the people got off. Timothy peeped out to look around. Wow! It looked as if he had arrived in rabbit heaven!

He jumped out the door to taste the bright green fern that was growing in neat rows. Sure enough, the fern tasted as good as it looked. Timothy was so happy! He was hopping up and down the rows of fern, taking a bite here and a nibble there. He had no idea that his trip had taken him all the way from Texas to a fiddle-head fern farm in Alaska!

Suddenly, he heard the people coming back to the bus. He hopped through the door and back to his hiding place in the sweater bag before anyone noticed him. As soon as all the people got back on, the bus again started down the road. Timothy was glad he hadn't missed the bus. He really liked traveling. He wondered why anyone would want to stay in one place all the time. There were so many interesting things to do and so many beautiful places to see in the world.

Timothy was feeling much braver. At the next stop he even got out and had his picture taken, just as the other tourists did.

When the people started coming back to the bus, Timothy was always the first one on board. But Timothy became so bold that he began to get careless. The next time the tour stopped for pie and coffee, Timothy could hardly wait to hop out and nibble on the tasty green fern.

Then he noticed some interesting red berries beside a tall pine tree. He just had to taste them too. He couldn't decide which he liked the best.

All at once he heard a familiar sound. His bus was pulling out of the parking lot. Timothy hopped after it as fast as he could. He wanted to

yell, "Wait for me!" But he couldn't make a sound. He followed the bus down the road until it was completely out of sight.

Timothy sat down in the middle of the road and began to cry. But he didn't cry very long. With a deafening roar like a tornado, a giant truck went speeding past him. The huge wheels passed within inches of his furry little tail. A great gust of wind blew him right off the road and into a low cranberry bush.

Timothy decided to hop into the woods to hide. He found a patch of fireweed higher than his head and sat down to think about what he should do next.

Timothy began to shiver. It would be dark soon. And it would probably be cold here after the sun went down. He wondered if there were any big animals around looking for a rabbit for their dinner.

Then he heard a peculiar sound. It was a sound he had never heard before. Timothy was very curious. Slowly and quietly, he made his way toward the sound.

A boy was sitting in front of a small
homemade cross. He was sobbing so loudly that
he didn't even notice Timothy.

Timothy came closer and closer. He was so close his whiskers were almost tickling the boy's elbow. The boy still didn't notice Timothy.

Timothy twitched his nose and wiggled his whiskers, trying to get the boy's attention. But the boy just kept right on crying. Finally, Timothy gathered up his courage and jumped right into the boy's lap. The boy quit crying and

opened his eyes. He was so surprised to find a bunny in his lap that he forgot all about being sad. First he smiled. Then he laughed as Timothy's whiskers tickled his hand.

"What a brave bunny you are," he said.
"You are not a bit afraid of me." He held the
bunny for a long time.

"I'd like to take you home with me," the
boy said sadly, "but you are a wild animal. I've
always heard that all wild animals should live
out in the woods and be free." The boy began
walking slowly down the trail.

Timothy started hopping along after him. He didn't want to live wild and free. He only wanted a friend to love and take care of him.

When the boy stopped to turn around for one last look, he almost stepped on Timothy. "My goodness," he said, "it seems like you want to tag along with me. Would you like to be my pet?"

Timothy tried to say, "Yes, yes!" He was so excited. He began to tremble.

"You must be cold," said the boy. "Hop inside my backpack. It's nice and warm in there."

"I must give you a name," said the boy. "What shall I call such a brave little animal? I could call you Brave Benny Bunny or Courageous Charlie Cottontail or even Tagging Along Thomas, but none of those names seem to fit. I know! I'll call you Tag-Along Timothy. You can follow me everywhere. We will have wonderful adventures together."

Timothy was so happy. He would never be ashamed to be called Tag-Along again. He snuggled up next to his new friend, and they went off toward their home in Alaska together.